Meet Thor

Written by Brooke Vitale

Illustrated by the Marvel Storybook Artists

marvelkids.com

Printed in China

First Box Set Edition, September 2017

7 9 10 8 6

FAC-025393-21011

ISBN 978-1-368-01613-1

This is Thor.

Thor is from the planet Asgard.

Thor has a brother.
His name is Loki.

Thor has a magic hammer.

Thor uses his power
to help people.

Thor protects Earth with the Avengers. He is a hero.